The FROG FILES

Annie Dalton

Illustrated by Brett Hudson

mammoth

*For my daughter Maria with love and thanks.
And in loving memory of Christine Shiu,
frog-maths expert and friend.*

A.D.

First published in Great Britain in 2000
by Mammoth, an imprint of Egmont Children's Books Limited
239 Kensington High Street, London W8 6SA

Text copyright © 2000 Annie Dalton
Illustrations copyright © 2000 Brett Hudson

The moral rights of the author and illustrator have been asserted.

The rights of Annie Dalton and Brett Hudson to be
identified as the author and illustrator of this work have been asserted by
them in accordance with the Copyright, Designs and Patents Act 1988

ISBN 0 7497 3654 2

10 9 8 7 6 5 4 3 2

A CIP catalogue record for this book
is available from the British Library

Printed in Great Britain
by Cox & Wyman Ltd, Reading, Berkshire

Contents

~

1. Blat! Blat! Blat!

Spring had arrived in Darkwoods. Birds shouted from rooftops. Weeds poked through the concrete. And Tyler wanted to go to school about as much as he wanted chickenpox.

When he finally dragged himself upstairs to his classroom, Cory was glaring out of the window, chewing his nails.

'What's up?' Tyler asked.

'Angie Fern's late,' sighed Jade.

Ricardo scowled. 'Bet she's left to teach at some posh school.'

'Why does everyone hate Darkwoods kids so much?' asked Sita.

'They think we've got brains like peanuts,' Ali explained.

'But Angie's different,' said Ying Lee.

'Shut up,' said Cory. 'Just shut *up*.'

Suddenly they heard the familiar roar of a motorbike. Seconds later, Angie Fern appeared, carrying a muddy primrose in a pot. 'Sorry, guys,' she beamed. 'Bike trouble.' She plunked down the primrose and unzipped her leather jacket. Spring sunlight glinted off her nose-stud.

'Open the windows and get some oxygen into those wonderful brains of yours,' she said briskly. 'I want you to do brilliantly in today's test.'

Tyler sagged with despair. School was heaps more exciting with Angie to teach them, but it was really hard work. They had a maths test every single Friday. And no

matter how hard he tried, Tyler never got more than two out of twenty.

At the end of the lesson, Angie found him staring glumly at his test paper.

'You'll get the hang of it, Tyler,' she told him. 'You need to relax.'

I need a teeny weeny genius in my pocket to tell me all the answers, he thought. *That's* what I need.

The spring weather made Angie's class more fidgety than usual. To calm them down, she opened the book of fairytales and chose a story at random. It was called

'The Frog Prince'. The children listened to her in astonished silence. Then Cory patted her arm.

'No offence, Miss, but that's a rubbish story.'

'It doesn't make sense,' agreed Tanisha. 'She only kissed the frog because her dad made her.'

'What was she doing, anyway, chucking a solid gold ball about near some old well?' said Jade scornfully.

Cory tapped his nose. 'If you ask me, they left something out. Something they didn't want us to know.'

Ying Lee giggled. 'You sound like a detective.'

'Detectives are ace!' said Ricardo. 'They blow cars up. KERBOOM!'

I wish I was a detective, thought Tyler. They understand everything – even maths.

Angie clapped her hands. 'By amazing coincidence we're going to do some detective work this afternoon.'

'Yeah, right,' grinned Cory.

'I'm serious. Scientists look for clues and solve problems, just like detectives.' Angie smiled at them. 'We're going on a field trip.'

'Fields? Round here?' said Owen.

'I thought we'd take a look at that wasteland behind the box factory,' said Angie. 'I've asked the council to let us use it as a nature area.'

Ricardo yawned. 'Nature's boring.'

'Why, because it doesn't go "Kerboom!"?' sneered Jade.

After dinner, the class walked down to the box factory to see Angie's nature area. Tyler wasn't impressed. There was nothing to see, except a scummy pond with junk bobbing

around in it. The children peered into the water. 'Yuk,' said Jade.

'We'll clean it out,' said Angie. 'We'll plant trees and flowers. It'll be wonderful, you'll see.'

Cory scowled. 'You're wasting your time, Miss. The minute you turn your back, the big kids will rip out your pretty trees and chuck the rubbish straight back in the pond.'

'This estate's a dump, Miss,' said Ali. 'Some wicked people live here.'

'Yeah, you can't change that, Miss,' said Tanisha.

WHOOSH! A tingle of electricity whizzed up Tyler's spine and, before he knew it, he was sounding off like an expert on telly. 'Darkwoods wasn't always like this,' he said. 'Flats and flyovers. Car chases and robberies. Once upon a time, there used to be –'

Stop, sto-op, he told himself frantically. The Darkwoods magic was his special secret. Once all the other children knew, he'd be just like everyone else.

The whole class was staring at him. Suddenly the air was fizzy with enchantment.

The magic *wants* me to tell them, he thought.

'Once upon a time . . . ?' Ying Lee prompted.

'There used to be woods,' he said huskily.

'Big dark woods, where those old fairytales happened. They chopped down the trees. But they couldn't get rid of the magic.'

'You mean the beanstalk wasn't a one-off?' Cory looked astounded.

'Uh-uh,' said Tyler. 'There's plenty more magic where that came from.'

'If we clean the pond, will the magic come back?' asked Sita.

Tyler nodded. 'Maybe.'

'I'll help then,' offered Owen.

'Me too,' said Jade.

Ricardo and Ali started dragging bits of old bed out of the water.

Angie laughed. 'It's Saturday tomorrow. Put your old clothes and wellies on and come and

8

help me then. For now, let's do the detective work and see how many different plants we can find.'

Everyone wandered off, chattering excitedly.

Only Tyler stayed by the pond, as if he'd been glued there. The Darkwoods magic was on the move. He could feel it fizzing under his feet, like a water-main getting ready to burst. The pond began to froth and bubble. Help! thought Tyler.

Suddenly, he heard a splash a few metres behind him, followed by sinister squishing sounds. Blat! Blat! Blat!

Tyler didn't know what to do. If he turned round, he might see a terrifying monster. If he didn't, the monster could creep up behind him on its squishy feet and –

'Tyler?' said a hoarse voice. 'Tyler Rapido?'

Tyler's knees turned to jelly. *The monster knew his name.* Slowly, slowly, he swivelled round. And found himself looking at a large frog.

Tyler took a horrified step backwards, tripped over a rusty bed spring and fell sprawling. The frog stared at him with bright bulging eyes. 'Am I addressing the right person?' it inquired politely.

Apart from sounding like a gangster, it was just like an ordinary frog. In fact, as frogs went, it was probably quite good looking. It's just that frogs totally gave Tyler the creeps. *Talking* frogs gave him the creeps times about a zillion.

'I need your help,' said the frog. 'A great wrong has been committed.'

Tyler still felt queasy. 'A  wrong?' he echoed. 'What kind of wrong?'

The frog placed a froggy finger to its lips. 'It's better if we talk at your place,' it said. 'If my case interests you, maybe you'll take it on.'

Tyler picked himself up. 'I don't take on cases,' he said. 'I'm a kid.'

'Wait till you've heard the deal. You're going to love it, Rapido. Trust me.' The frog stretched its mouth into a hideous smile.

'I don't do deals with frogs either.' Tyler didn't mean to be rude. The words just splurted out.

The frog was silent so long, Tyler guessed it was sulking.

'I could have offered this case to any private eye in the business,' it said at last. 'But I didn't. Why? I'll tell you. Rapido's one of the good guys, they said. He's the

11

best. He'll give you a chance. Huh!'

The frog hopped very slowly towards the pond. It seemed to have acquired a limp. 'Have a nice life,' it said bitterly.

'Oh, all right,' Tyler sighed. The frog whipped round, miraculously regaining full use of its limbs. 'You'll take me home?' it cried.

'You're not sharing my plate, OK,' said Tyler. 'You're certainly not sharing my pillow. And I'm most definitely NOT kissing you!'

'You won't regret it!' The frog dived joyously into Tyler's pocket.

Tyler's sisters followed him through the front door. As well as her school pinafore, Simone wore Tyler's old cap, a long glittery scarf and clashing socks. Mum had let her dress herself for school again today. 'You're walking funny, Ty,' she giggled, spluttering sherbet everywhere.

'So would you, if you had a frog in your pocket,' he growled.

Next minute the frog pinged through the air like a rubber band, landing neatly by the telephone. 'Your office is a little cramped, Rapido,' it remarked. 'Times must be hard, huh?'

Simone's mouth fell open. 'He can talk! That's so cute! Can we keep him!'

Tyler sighed. 'It's not an office,' he said. 'It's just our hall.'

The frog noticed Tyler's big sister Rose. It edged closer. 'Are you a princess, by any chance, Miss?' it asked.

'No, that's just Rose,' Tyler said. 'The

short sherbety one is Simone.'

'Perhaps Rose would like to hear my story too?' The frog puckered its lips hopefully.

Rose gave a vague smile. 'Thanks, but I've got stuff to do.'

Things were definitely getting out of hand. 'Let's go up to my room,' said Tyler quickly. The frog hopped after him, landing on each step with a clammy thud. Blat! Blat! Blat!

Tyler shut the door. Before he could open his mouth, the frog was pouring its heart out.

'The moment I saw her, I knew she was the one I'd been waiting for. She said she felt the same. But when I turned up at the palace, she told the king she'd never seen me before in her life. Something fishy is going on, Rapido. I might act tough. And I might talk tough. But my heart is breaking here.' The frog's face crumpled like an old boot.

'You mentioned a deal,' prompted Tyler.

The frog's eyes bulged like headlamps.  'A teeny weeny genius to tell you all the answers. Wasn't that what you wished for? Just think, Rapido! Twenty out of twenty in those maths tests for ever and ever!'

Tyler gulped. 'Do you mean it?' he whispered.

'All I'm asking is one weekend out of your life,' said the frog. 'One measly weekend.'

Tyler struggled with his conscience for almost half a second. 'Done,' he said.

2. Front-page frog

Next morning, Tyler didn't jump out of bed right away. He lay under his quilt thinking happy Saturday thoughts. But finally his belly growled for breakfast, so he went downstairs.

Mum was in the kitchen. 'It's a scandal,' she said. 'Some people think they can get away with murder.'

Tyler sloshed milk on his cereal, only half listening. 'Mmm,' he mumbled.

Then he saw Mum's paper. FROG TELLS

ALL blared the headline. Underneath was a face like a crumpled old boot.

Tyler's heart missed a beat. That slimy frog had snitched to the papers about their secret bargain! *I haven't even done anything wrong. Not yet, anyway,* he told himself. *So there was absolutely no reason to feel guilty.* Tyler scanned the front page to see if it mentioned a well-known local maths cheat.

To his surprise, Mum gave him a hug. 'I'm so proud of you!' she said. 'It's time someone stood up to that royal family.'

Tyler stared at her. 'Did Simone tell you about the frog?' he asked nervously.

Mum beamed. 'As if Simone would blab a client's private business. No, it's right here at the bottom of the page! "Tyler Rapido, champion of the underdog",' she read out.

'Why did they say that?'

asked Tyler bewildered. 'And it's not a dog, it's a frog.'

Mum finished her coffee. 'Better run. Don't want to get fired, my first day at the palace.'

Tyler was totally confused now. 'Palace?' he said. 'You don't work at any palace, Mum. You work at Rainbow House. And you never ever work on Saturdays. You promised, remember?'

Mum sighed. 'Honey, that mean old king and queen own this whole estate. Everybody works for them. And when you work for royalty, it makes no difference what day it is. If they say work, you *work*.' She grabbed her coat and hurried out.

Front page frogs? Selfish kings and queens running Darkwoods? Tyler needed a nice long shower to help him recover. But even with gallons of hot water thundering down on top of his head, Tyler couldn't switch off his brain. It buzzed with questions.

What if the frog had lied to him? Why had it spilled its beans to the press, when yesterday it acted like it was telling Tyler a great big secret? And how come even Tyler's mum seemed to believe her son ran some kind of detective agency?

He wrapped himself in a towel and padded into his room to get dressed. He opened his cupboard to get his jogging bottoms, but all his clothes had vanished. Instead, Tyler was staring at a row of sharp Italian suits.

'Oh, boy,' he whispered. 'I really *am* a detective.'

The suits were Tyler's size exactly. He put one on. In the top pocket he found a pair of sunglasses.

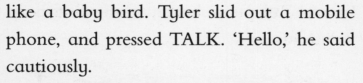

He was just admiring himself in the mirror when his trousers began to chirp like a baby bird. Tyler slid out a mobile phone, and pressed TALK. 'Hello,' he said cautiously.

'Your client is waiting,' said a voice.

'Simone?' said Tyler amazed. 'What are you doing on my phone?'

'I'm your sidekick, Rapido,' said his little sister. 'Your brilliant but wacky assistant. You'd better come down right away. Your client seems *very* upset.'

Tyler took a deep breath. 'Where are you, exactly?'

'Look out of the window,' she said in her crisp assistant's voice. He dragged back the curtains. Simone waved from the garden shed. 'Don't worry,' she said in his ear. 'I remembered the coffee and doughnuts.'

Tyler detested coffee. He started to say so, but Simone had already rung off. Almost immediately, his phone chirped again.

Tyler answered it and got an unpleasant surprise. 'Rapido?' barked his headmaster.

'Sir?' Tyler stammered.

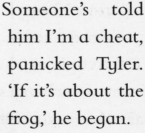

'What do you think you're up to?'

Someone's told him I'm a cheat, panicked Tyler. 'If it's about the frog,' he began.

'You bet it's

about the frog,' raged Mr Scrim. 'The frog is trouble. Trouble gives me indigestion. And when I've got indigestion, I'm not a happy police inspector.'

'Right,' said Tyler cautiously. He had no idea why Mr Scrim was pretending to be a police inspector, but he wasn't going to argue with him.

'Would it make any difference if I ordered you to drop this case?' Mr Scrim demanded.

'Erm,' said Tyler. 'I don't —'

Mr Scrim gave a grim chuckle. 'That's what I thought. You're a brave kid, Rapido. But I'm warning you. If you don't solve this case by Sunday night, I'll turn it over to my superiors.' The phone went dead.

Tyler dashed to the bottom of the garden. The Rapido's shed had undergone some interesting changes in the night. It was nearly as big as their house for one thing. Nailed to the wall was a battered sign:

22

RAPIDO & RAPIDO
PRIVATE INVESTIGATORS.

Tyler went inside and found Simone frowning at a computer screen. Now and then she tapped a key with one careful

finger. She had scraped her hair into a little bun. Her school pinafore was freshly ironed. Her socks matched perfectly. There was no sherbet anywhere.

'Simone,' he said in surprise. 'You're so — tidy.' She swivelled in her chair and Tyler saw a pencil skewered through her bun like an arrow.

'So you finally showed up,' she said. 'I've been here all night, checking through our files.' She took the pencil out of her hair and used it to stir her coffee. She had a new severe expression to match her voice.

Tyler suddenly noticed the frog perched on the edge of a chair. 'You saw today's papers, huh?' it said miserably.

'I thought it was a big secret. Me working for you,' said Tyler. 'In my family we don't blab our secrets to newspapers.'

Ooer, I'm acting really tough, he thought. Must be the suit.

'OK, so I went a little crazy,' agreed the frog tearfully. 'Maybe I was hoping that when she saw my story in the paper, she'd be sorry. Have a change of heart.'

'Did it work?' said Tyler.

The frog glared at him. 'Do you think I'd be here, bawling like a baby, if it had?' Then it buried its face in its hands and sobbed as if its heart would break.

Tyler gave his client a soothing pat. It felt every bit as creepy as he thought it would. 'You hired me to solve this case,' he said in a firm voice. 'So I'm going to solve it. But first we've got to –'

'– go back to the scene of the crime,' Simone interrupted.

'How did you know?' said Tyler, dying to wipe his hand on his suit.

Simone sighed. 'It's obvious. We've got to prove our client is telling the truth. That means we need evidence.'

His sister was being a proper little smarty-pants. Tyler decided to show her who was in charge.

'OK, let's go, let's go!' he said, like the detectives on telly. 'Want to jump in my pocket, frog?' he added bravely.

As they left the office, Angie Fern roared up on her bike. 'Thought you might need a lift,' she said.

Simone and the frog scrambled into her sidecar. Tyler hopped on behind Angie, and they zoomed off down the street.

Tyler was amazed at the changes which had taken place in Darkwoods while he was sleeping. A large hill had appeared, bang in the middle of his estate. It wasn't just any old hill either. Someone had taken a great deal of time and money to get it looking smooth and green.

A narrow white road wound its way twistily to the top, like a road in a fairytale. There, well away from the dirt and noise of Darkwoods, someone had built a palace, so pink Tyler could see it glowing amongst the trees.

But the palace didn't look anything like a fairytale palace. It had a whacking great satellite dish for one thing. 'Birthday cake!' muttered Tyler. 'A big stupid birthday cake. That's what it looks like.'

Poor frog, thought Tyler. It had hopped all that way to see him on its little webbed feet. And suddenly he was absolutely sure the frog was telling the truth about his meeting with the princess. Nobody would make such a painful journey if they didn't absolutely *have* to.

'I'll drop you here,' Angie yelled. 'See you later, guys.' Her passengers jumped down and Tyler's teacher went roaring off.

Tyler looked around in surprise. Angie's nature area looked like a scene from *Robin Hood*. The air smelled of wood-smoke. Scruffy tents had sprung up like mushrooms. And, high in a tree, some girls were building a rickety tree-house. A large dog ran round in circles, barking excitedly.

Tyler reached for Simone's hand. Dogs terrified her. But his little sister marched past without blinking.

When they reached the pond, Simone took out a magnifying glass and started crawling around in the dirt. Suddenly she gave a yelp and held something up for Tyler to see.

A gold ring sparkled on her palm.

'I remember now,' said the frog going all misty-eyed. 'That ring was the first thing I saw when I looked up at her through the water. It shone so brightly, I was completely dazzled.'

'Now the king will *have* to believe you,' said Simone.

Tyler could hardly believe it. His first day

of being a real detective and they'd cracked the case already!

The frog looked so dazed that Tyler gave it a comforting pat. This time it didn't feel quite so creepy. 'Did you hear what my assistant said?' he asked. 'We solved the case. You're going to live happily ever after!'

3. The golden rattle

The royal hill rose ahead of them, smooth as an egg and greener than a film star's lawn.

Their client had been unusually quiet on their long walk across Darkwoods to see the king. 'Don't you feel well?' Simone crooned. 'I'm trying not to bump you.'

The frog gave a weak smile. 'You guys solved my case so fast, I'm kind of dizzy.' Then it heaved a sigh. 'You're my friends. I can't lie to you. The truth is –' it swallowed. 'I'm not really a frog.'

Simone quickly dumped the frog on the grass. 'What are you then? An alien?'

'Don't ask! My former life is a blank.' The frog gazed miserably into space.

Poor frog. It's really forgotten who it is, thought Tyler. 'Tell us exactly what happened,' he said in his best detective's voice. He seated himself cosily next to the frog and tugged Simone down beside him.

The frog cleared its throat. 'Long, long ago,' it began, 'I woke from a deep sleep to find myself at the bottom of a pond. This felt kind of spooky, but I couldn't figure out why. I swam up to the top. It was night-time but the moon was bright. All at once I saw my reflection.' The frog shuddered.

'Now I looked like a frog. I could also

swim like a frog. And it's
not a nice thing to tell
you but, pretty soon, I
was even slurping up
slimy bugs and beetles
like a frog.'

Simone squeaked and covered her mouth.

'But I was absolutely one hundred percent
positive I was *not* a frog. However, I didn't
have a clue what to do about it. Then one
day I was mooching around in the mud
when a tiny voice spoke to me.'

'Was it a bug?' Simone asked, gulping.

'It was an *invisible* voice, deep inside me,'
the frog explained patiently. 'The voice said
it was my destiny to meet a beautiful
princess, who would help me solve my
difficulties. I just had to wait.'

'How long did you wait?' asked Tyler.

'A few hundred frog years,' the frog said
carelessly. 'Then, just a few days ago, a

bright object fell towards me through the water.'

'Not a UFO?' breathed Simone.

'It was a golden ball, bird-brain,' said Tyler.

The frog shook its head. 'It was a rattle. A golden rattle with precious jewels all over it. At first, I didn't think much of it. I don't want to offend you guys, but some humans, they see a pond and automatically they gotta dump all kinds of stuff in it. Anyway, time passed.'

Simone took out her notebook. 'Frog time or human time?'

The frog ignored her. 'Suddenly I heard splashing sounds. I looked up, but all I could see was light. Dazzling yellow light.'

Simone was scribbling furiously.

'Then someone called for help.' The frog gave a dreamy smile. 'What a sweet sound.

I went bombing to
the top of the pond.
And there she was,
fresh as a water lily.
"Can I assist you in
some way, Miss?" I
asked. She told me
someone stole a valuable plaything from her
baby brother and threw it in the pond. She
tried to fish it out, but the water was too
deep.'

Cory was right, thought Tyler. They left
loads out of this story.

' "It so happens I've got a serious problem
of my own, Miss", I told her. "Maybe we
can do a deal here".' The frog fell silent.

'So then you fetched her the rattle,'
prompted Tyler.

The frog didn't answer. 'You know what
really hurts?' it said at last. 'That first time,
beside the pond, she acted as if she liked me.

She even recited a poem for me. Then at the palace, she was like a completely different person. She –'

But at that moment Tyler's dad drove up in his taxi. He wound down the window. 'How's it going, kids?' he yelled.

'We cracked the case,' Tyler yelled back. 'We're going to tell the king.'

'Jump in!' Dad said. 'I'm going your way.'

'Don't let anyone see me till I'm ready,' hissed the frog.

'OK,' sighed Tyler. The frog dived into his pocket. Tyler and Simone got in the taxi and Dad drove off.

'Hiya,' said Dad's passenger. 'I'm Catkin.'

'Are you going to the palace, Catkin?' Tyler asked her.

She gave a mysterious smile. 'Kind of.'

In Tyler's opinion, Catkin should tidy herself up

before she went visiting royalty. Her clothes were mud-splattered. Her nose and left eyebrow were pierced and her embroidered cap had a dead leaf stuck to it. For some reason she was clutching a can of paint. Simone eyed her thoughtfully.

The road grew steeper. And when Tyler looked back, he noticed something strange. Down in Darkwoods, the weather was dull and cloudy. But high on the hill, the pink palace was bathed in perfect sunshine.

'Drop me here,' Catkin said suddenly. She patted her pockets. 'Wire cutters. Paint brush,' she murmured. 'Yep, I've got

everything.' She jumped out of the car and went snaking through the trees like a commando. Tyler stared after her. 'What's she up to?'

'The king wants to put a carpark on that wasteland near our house,' said Dad. 'But the eco-warriors found some rare bluebells there. Catkin's going to paint protest slogans on the palace.'

'I knew I'd seen her before,' said Simone. 'She was in that tree-house.'

The taxi stopped at some tall gates. Two enormous guards stepped out of nowhere. 'Up here again, Joe,' grinned one. 'What's Princess Ruby been buying this week? Itsy bitsy silk pyjamas? A cute little handbag the size of a postage stamp?'

'No royal shopping today,' Dad told them. 'A couple of famous detectives want to see the king on private business.'

The guards peered into the taxi. Tyler stared straight ahead, his heart thumping. 'It's them,' hissed the first guard. 'Tyler Rapido and his assistant. They must have got some new evidence.'

The other guard chuckled. 'Serves her right. Princesses shouldn't make promises they don't intend to keep.' He pressed a button and the royal gates swung open. The guards saluted as Tyler's dad drove through.

The gates closed behind them.

'I'll wait here,' said Dad.

The children found themselves in a tree-lined avenue. Bright sunlight spilled down on them. Tyler was getting uncomfortably hot inside his suit. 'How come the royal family gets different weather?' he said.

'It's not just the weather,' said Simone. She pointed.

Tyler stared up at the waving palm trees, amazed. These people are outrageous, he thought. A pink palace isn't enough for them. They've got to have their own private country as well!

As they reached the palace steps, a butler scurried out. He whisked them down gleaming corridors, and past rooms full of gold-painted furniture. Finally a pair of doors was flung open and Tyler and Simone followed him out into a tropical afternoon.

A girl floated on her back in a dazzling

40

blue pool. Beside the
pool, under a giant
umbrella, the king
and queen sipped
at tall glasses
clinking with ice.
Nearby, a hot-
looking baby grizzled
in its cradle.

'This had better be good, Rapido,'
grumbled the king.

Tyler handed over the ring. 'The princess
dropped this beside the pond,' he said.

The king turned pale. 'I – er – I,' he said.
Then he pulled himself together. 'It does
have the royal
seal on it,' he
admitted huskily.
'My dear,' he said
to his wife. 'We
may have to –'

'Piffle,' interrupted the queen. 'Ruby!' she squawked. 'Come here!'

The girl swam sulkily to the side of the pool. 'What?' she demanded.

'These detectives say they've found your ring. They think it proves that creature's ridiculous story.'

Princess Ruby lifted a slender arm out of the water. An identical ring sparkled on her hand.

'What a hoot,' she said. 'But, as you can see, I've still got mine.'

Tyler's pocket gave a lurch. The frog sprang on to the table. The queen shrieked with horror.

'She's lying!' cried the frog. 'She said my eyes were beautiful.'

He swung to face the princess, his headlamp eyes blazing. 'Why did you say those things if you didn't mean them?' he

demanded. 'Does a
frog have no feelings?
No soul?'

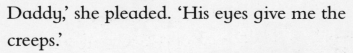

Princess Ruby
clambered quickly out of
the pool. 'Don't listen,
Daddy,' she pleaded. 'His eyes give me the
creeps.'

The king scowled. 'This nonsense has
gone on long enough, Ruby,' he snapped. 'I
had this ring specially made for you. I don't
know what you were up to, down by the
pond, but you obviously lost your ring and
got our jeweller to make you a copy.'

'I didn't!' the princess wailed. 'Daddy,
you've got to believe me.'

The king ignored her. 'You have my word
that her royal highness will keep her
promises to you,' he told the frog. He glared
at his daughter. 'Or I'll stop her pocket
money!'

The king picked up the baby. 'I'm taking Garnet inside,' he told his wife. 'He's melting. Yes you are, precious diddums.'

'Mummy, it's not fair,' complained the princess. 'Daddy's so mean since Pearl –'

But Tyler wasn't listening to the spoiled princess. His adventure was over at last. He could stop being a hardworking detective and mess about on his bike for the rest of the weekend, like a normal kid.

And you know what? He couldn't wait!

4. Everything goes VROOM!

Tyler went to bed in a great mood. Any minute now, the princess would kiss the frog, just like in Angie's story, and VROOM! There'd be a massive flash of lightning and Darkwoods would go back to normal.

He drifted into a deep sleep. He was doing a humungously hard maths test. But a baby bird chirped so loudly, Tyler couldn't hear himself think.

Tyler woke up. The chirping carried on. He fumbled in the dark and found his phone. 'Hello,' he croaked.

'Our client just walked back in,' said Simone. 'Oh, and Inspector Scrim is here.'

Tyler banged his head against the wall. I don't want to be a detective, he thought. I want to be a kid. He put on his clothes and went out into the night.

Inspector Scrim had his feet on the desk. He dunked a stale doughnut in his coffee and slurped at it. 'I warned you, Rapido,' he growled.

Tyler felt bewildered. 'But the king said —'

The frog came out of the shadows. 'It didn't work out,' it said bitterly.

Tyler tried desperately to think like a detective. 'You're sure you did everything you were supposed to?' he asked.

The frog sighed. 'Yeah, yeah. I had a bite from her royal chocolate eclair. And she let me share her royal pillow during her siesta, so long as I stayed on my own side. Her perfume made my eyes water,' it added gloomily.

'Didn't the princess let you kiss her?' asked Tyler indignantly.

'Sure I kissed her. Her lipstick tastes like Jelly Tots,' it said in disgust.

'But you're still a frog!' said Tyler.

The frog slumped against the wall. 'You noticed.'

'But everything's supposed to go VROOM!' whispered Tyler.

Inspector Scrim gave one of his grim chuckles. 'Good luck, Rapido. You'll need it.' He strode out of the office.

I give up, thought Tyler. He grabbed a stale doughnut and bit into it.

Simone frowned. 'I've been thinking. I know Ruby is really vain and shallow and everything, but I think she's telling the truth. She really didn't make those promises.'

The frog slid to the floor. 'Great!' it muttered. 'Not only am I trapped inside this slimy frog suit, but I'm a liar as well.'

'Actually,' said Simone calmly. 'I think you're telling the truth too.'

Tyler slapped himself across the head. 'Yippy skippy!' he said. 'I've got it! Princess Ruby's got a twin sister no one's allowed to talk about. The whole thing's been a HUGE mistake!'

Simone gasped. 'Rapido, you're a genius!' she squealed. 'Ruby didn't make those promises. It was her secret twin!'

Tyler sighed. 'I was just kidding, Simone.'

'No, listen.' She scrolled excitedly through her notes. ' "She was like a completely different person",' she read out.

The frog lifted its head, groggily. 'Are you saying there are TWO princesses?'

Suddenly Tyler started to pace up and down, talking at lightning speed, like a detective who has almost solved a case.

'Here's what happened. When the baby came along, Ruby was incredibly jealous. So she stole one of the christening presents and threw it in the pond. Her twin guessed what she was up to and ran after her. Ruby had calmed down by this time. They tried to fish the rattle out. But Ruby gave up and went home.'

'Then my princess called for help,' the frog whispered.

'The king *knew* it was her ring,' said Simone. 'He just pretended he didn't. Hmmm,' she said thoughtfully. 'I wonder why he did that?'

'Who cares?' said Tyler.

'Oops, I just kissed the wrong princess!' said the frog.

Tyler grinned happily. So what if he'd solved the mystery by accident? He felt brilliant. 'All we've got to do is find that twin,' he said.

Simone wilted against her computer. 'Do we have to start now?'

Tyler patted the top of her head. 'Take a nap, Miss Rapido. We'll start the twin hunt tomorrow.' He turned shyly to the frog. 'Could you help me with something? Unless you're tired?'

'Tired? I'm on top of the world!' the frog sang out.

Hours later Tyler opened his eyes. Sheets of paper covered his desk, each one covered in exquisite frog mathematics. The frog was a wizard at maths. And by the time he'd finished his midnight lesson, Tyler was pretty hot himself.

He left the others asleep and went home to shower and change.

As he came out of his room, he almost bumped into his big sister. He hardly recognised her. Her hair was twisted into springy dreads, and instead of jeans she wore baggy army trousers.

'Rose?' he said.

'Ssh! I'm helping with the protest,' she hissed. 'You know, to save the bluebells.' She stopped halfway down the stairs. 'How's your case going?'

'It's OK, now we've figured out the princess had a twin sister,' he whispered. 'But if we don't find her we're in big trouble.'

Rose gazed up at him thoughtfully. 'Come along to the camp later,' she said at last. 'I know someone who might be able to help. Can't promise anything though.'

So, after breakfast, they went to find Rose. The eco-warriors had been working hard. Every last weed and bit of rubbish had gone. Tyler could see his face in the pond.

Rose dropped out of a tree beside him. 'I'll introduce you to my friend,' she said. They ducked under the branches. A home-made sign said:

SAVE THE DARKWOODS BLUEBELLS.

The bluebells made a misty sweet-scented pool. In the middle of the flowers, a girl sat murmuring poetry to herself. The frog's lips moved as if it had heard the poem somewhere before.

'Aren't they lovely,' said the girl suddenly. 'They were hidden under the rubbish. It's so great that everybody is, like, getting together to save them at last.'

Apart from the paint smudges, she looked cleaner than the last time Tyler saw her. But her cap still had a dead leaf stuck to it. 'Catkin?' he said.

'Actually, no,' said Catkin surprisingly. 'I'm the person you're looking for. You know, the missing twin? My real name is Pearl. Mum's got a thing about jewels. I prefer trees and flowers. That's why I changed it when I ran away from home.'

'How come you're telling us all of a sudden?' asked Simone suspiciously.

The princess sighed. 'I still want to be an eco-warrior and everything, but I really miss Mum and Dad. I mean, peace and love begin on your own doorstep, right?'

The frog cleared its throat. 'Remember

me?' it said huskily.

Catkin's face lit up. 'Froggie! How are you doing, man?'

The frog stared at the ground. 'I went to the palace. But you weren't there.'

Catkin's hand flew to her mouth. 'This is so terrible! You see when I got home, there was this, like, huge row. Dad said I had to start acting like a real princess. Like Ruby, he meant.' She pulled a face. 'I said he needn't think he could push me around just because he was the stupid king.'

Simone's eyes were like saucers. 'Boy, I bet he was *really* mad then.'

'You're not kidding. He said that if I carried on defying his wishes, nobody in Darkwoods would even be allowed to mention my name. It would be as if I didn't exist. But I was so angry I didn't care. I stuffed some clothes in a bag and ran away to join the eco-warriors. I got so excited about saving the planet, I forgot all about you.'

'Oh, well. Who needs frogs?' said the frog bitterly.

'For pete's sake,' said Tyler. 'Stop sulking and kiss her.'

The frog blinked in surprise. 'But –'

'Just KISS her, OK?' yelled Simone.

The frog hopped on to Catkin's palm. Tyler shut his eyes.

VROOM! Lightning flashed. Three kinds of lightning. Pink, white and lavender zigzag.

Catkin giggled. 'Froggie, this is so cool.'

Tyler opened his eyes. A young man in muddy clothes grinned back.

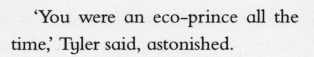

'You were an eco-prince all the time,' Tyler said, astonished.

Froggie looked embarrassed. 'That's not quite true,' he said. 'I was an extremely selfish youth. Chopping down trees. Polluting streams. But my years as a frog taught me to care about nature.' He went down on one knee. 'Catkin, will you marry me?'

Catkin threw her arms round him. 'I love you, man!'

Simone nudged Tyler. 'Let's go home and close the frog files,' she whispered.

That afternoon, Tyler's mobile phone rang for the very last time.

'Guess what!' said Catkin. 'I rang Dad and we've totally

made up. He said the palace was really boring without me there to keep him on his toes! Also, it turns out Froggie's dad is one of Dad's old school friends! Can you believe that? Dad's so thrilled about the wedding, he's throwing a huge party. You're all invited!'

It was a brilliant party. Tyler's family were guests of honour. Tyler's mum looked heaps nicer than the queen, who wore so much jewellery it was a wonder she could walk. And all Tyler's school friends were there. Tyler ate so much he thought his suit would split. He'd have eaten a whole lot more, but people kept coming up to congratulate him. 'Always knew you'd do it, Rapido,' said Inspector Scrim gruffly.

Tyler finally ran into Angie Fern by the chocolate eclairs. 'Well done, Tyler,' she grinned. 'The king's so happy he's promised to leave the bluebells for everyone to enjoy.'

But Tyler couldn't look Angie in the eye. Hey, it's not like I actually cheated, he thought crossly. He wanted to clear things up, just the same. 'Miss,' he stammered. 'I've been practising and I think I've got the hang of maths now. Actually I think maths is quite cool.'

'Excellent,' smiled Angie. 'Now, how about a dance!'

Tyler must have dozed off before the party was over because next thing he knew it was Monday morning. He 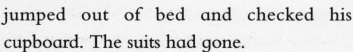 jumped out of bed and checked his cupboard. The suits had gone.

He peered out of his window. The private eye's office was shed-sized again. Then Tyler checked the landing window, just to make

sure. But the royal hill had vanished for ever.

'Tyler!' yelled Mum. 'Your sister's driving me crazy! Help her get ready for school!'

Tyler found Simone stumbling around in a panic. 'My feet don't work!' she wailed. Tyler quickly switched her trainers round. And for the zillionth time he showed her how to tie her laces.

'Simone,' he said thoughtfully. 'Pearl looks

like Maid Marion and Ruby looks like Barbie. How come the frog ever mixed them up?'

'That's easy,' she explained. 'Frogs don't have a clue about fashion.' His ex-assistant smiled her sweetest smile. 'Ty, I'm really really REALLY tired. Will you do my laces?' she pleaded. 'Plea-ase?'

'All right,' sighed Tyler. 'Just this once.'